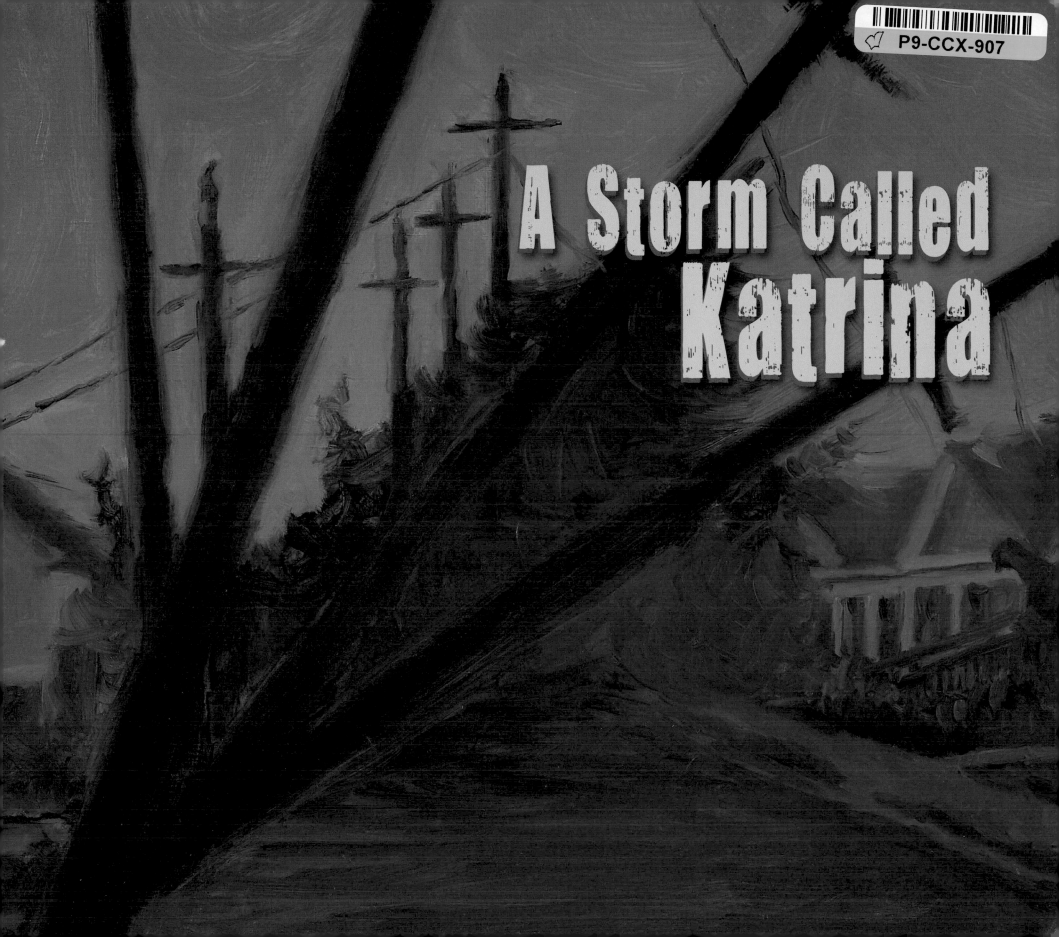

A Storm Called Katrina

A Storm Called Katrina

WRITTEN BY
Myron Uhlberg

ILLUSTRATED BY
Colin Bootman

PEACHTREE
ATLANTA

"HURRICANE'S COMING, Baby," Mama said.

"I'm not a baby anymore, Mama. I turned ten last month."

"Doesn't matter how old you are, Louis Daniel. You'll always be my baby," she said. "Hush now and go to bed."

The wind rattled my window something fierce. When the storm howled louder, I covered my ears and hid under the blanket.

I hugged my brass cornet close to my chest. I always feel better having it nearby. Someday I want to play just like Louis Daniel Armstrong—the greatest horn player ever.

In the morning, I saw that the storm had blown down our big oak tree with the tire swing. Mama's elephant ear plants were beaten flat to the ground.

"Will you look at that rain," Daddy said. Those drops were bigger than quarters. The wind slammed them sideways against the window.

Daddy pulled me away from the glass. The whole house shook.

"Don't you worry now," Mama said. "After some huffin' and puffin', Katrina will blow away and land up the coast just like all those other hurricanes."

But I couldn't stop worrying.

Finally the rain stopped, and everything got real quiet.

Daddy opened the door. "Water's rising fast," he said. "We've got to get out of here."

"Let me run and get a few things first," Mama said.

Daddy shook his head. "There's no time. It's already up to our front stoop."

I grabbed my horn from the coffee table. No way I was gonna leave it behind.

Outside, the world had turned upside down. Our whole block was filling up with water.

"Levee's broke!" a man behind us shouted. "Everybody head south!"

I held onto Mama and my horn as tight as I could.

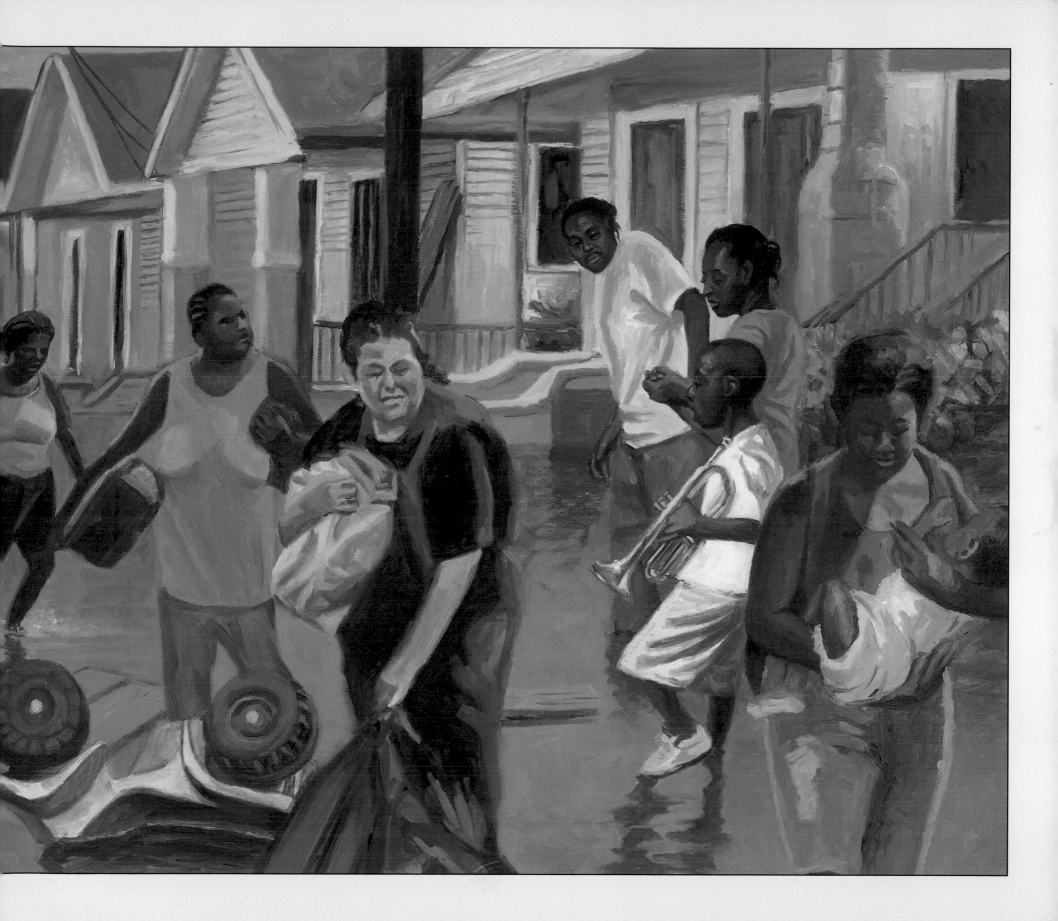

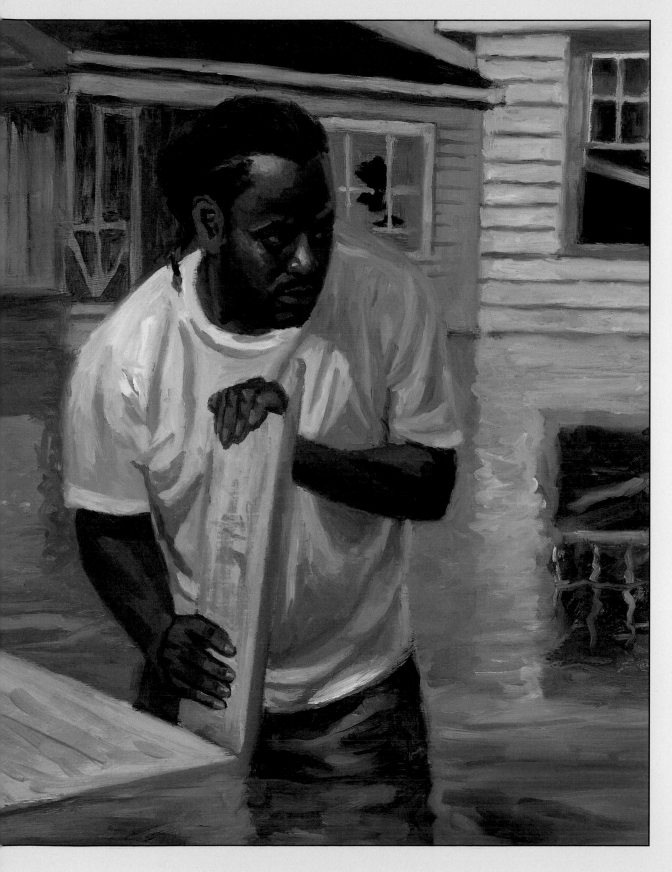

The water rose so high that we had trouble walking.

Daddy grabbed a piece of someone's porch that was floating by and lifted me up onto it. I was glad, 'cause I was afraid we might run into a gator. I kept a sharp watch, just in case.

Mama climbed up beside me and held me in her arms. "Everything's going to be fine, Baby," she said.

I almost didn't mind her calling me Baby just then.

As Daddy pushed us along, all kinds of things drifted by, even somebody's plastic Christmas tree.

I saw a sad-looking dog standing on a bunch of boards. He had a red ball in his mouth.

"Daddy," I said. "Can we take him with us?"

"No, Louis," he said.

The dog wagged his tail, like he wanted to play. He never stopped looking at me as we floated past.

I sure felt sorry for that dog. He was in the same fix we were.

The water was up to Daddy's chest by now. The sky was so blue and bright it hurt my eyes.

Daddy pushed that big old piece of porch up one street and down the next.

I tried to help by paddling with a broom that I pulled out of the water.

A flatboat floated by.

"Got any room for us?" Daddy called to the driver.

"Sorry," the man said. "We're full."

"Please, mister," I said. "There's a black and white dog back there. Can you take him? He's not very big."

The man didn't answer. The boat just drifted away.

The murky brown water rose so high
Daddy had to climb up on the porch boat
with Mama and me. That was when my
broom hit a pile of clothes. Mama covered
my eyes. "Don't look, Baby," she said.

But I couldn't help looking.

We rowed and paddled until we reached a place where the water wasn't as deep. Daddy jumped off and began to push us again. Finally, we felt the bottom of our boat scrape the ground. Mama and I got off, too.

"Where do we go now?" I asked.
"I don't know, Baby," Mama said.

We joined a long line of folks heading toward the Superdome. Everyone said we'd be safe there.

When we got closer, I could see that the storm had torn away part of the Dome's big white roof. People were shouting and crowding toward the gates.

A lady dragging a garbage bag full of stuff came up to us. "I've lived around these parts for fifty years," she said, "and I ain't never seen nothin' like this." She hoisted the heavy bag over her shoulder. "I just didn't reckon the storm would ever get this bad."

Mama shook her head. "Nobody did."

The Superdome was a lot bigger inside than it looked on TV. Sunlight streamed through holes in the roof.

Thousands of people were spread all over the place. The air was hot and stinky.

Mama, Daddy, and me searched until we found an empty row of seats, then sat down to wait.

I was tired and hungry and wished we could go home. I kept thinking about that little black and white dog.

I wondered if he was all right.

When the electricity went out, Mama, Daddy, and me huddled close together in the dark. I was scared, but I finally fell asleep.

In the middle of the night, I woke up from a bad dream about losing my cornet. I felt better when I saw that it was still tucked next to Mama.

But I couldn't get back to sleep. Babies were crying and people were talking. Some folks were yelling at each other.

The next day it got even hotter. People had to wait in long lines for the bathrooms. When we finally got in, it smelled so bad I had to hold my breath.

On the way back to our seats, we heard someone say that food and water were running out.

Daddy thought he'd better try to find us something to eat, and maybe some more water. "Louis," he said. "Keep an eye on your mama. I'll be back as soon as I can."

Daddy didn't come back all that afternoon.

Two men in front of us started fighting over a water bottle. The first man saw me watching them. "Hey, boy," he said, eyeing the bottle in my hand. "Give me that!"

"Leave my son alone," Mama said. She stood up and hustled us right out of our seats.

"Come on," she said. "We're going to sit somewhere else."

"But what about Daddy?" I asked, grabbing my cornet. "He won't be able to find us."

"Yes, he will, Baby," Mama said. "Don't you worry."

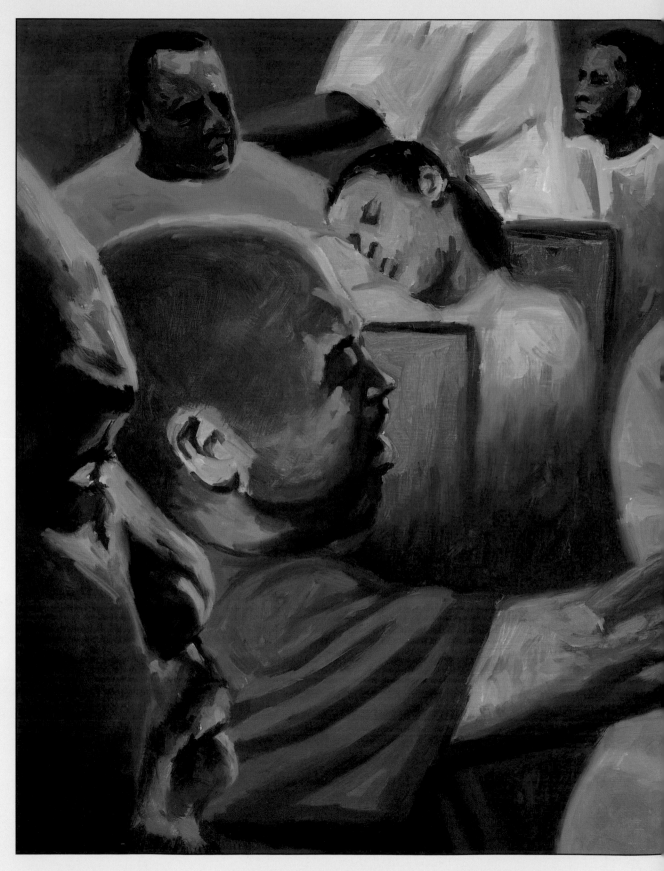

We waited in our new seats...then waited some more. My legs hurt from sitting so long. Mama seemed tired and worried.

I looked all around that huge Dome. *There are too many people crowded in this place*, I thought. *Daddy'll never find us now.*

I picked up my cornet and fingered the shiny buttons. That's when I had the idea.

"Mama," I said, jumping up. "I'll be right back."

"No, Baby, you stay right here."

"But, Mama, I know how to find Daddy."

She looked at me hard. "All right, but you come straight back. We're in Section 145, Row 23. Can you remember that?"

I nodded and took off down the stairs.

I hurried across the fake green grass and stopped right in the middle of the field. I closed my eyes, lifted my horn, and played a song my granddaddy had taught me, "Home, Sweet Home."

After I blew the last note, I stood there for a minute.

A voice cut through all the noise in the Superdome.

"LOUIS! LOUIS DANIEL!"

Daddy!

He ran all the way down the steps from the top of the Superdome. He grabbed me up in his arms and swung me around and around.

"I've looked all over this place," Daddy said. "I thought I'd never find you. Where's your mama?"

"Section 145," I answered. "Row 23."

When we got back, Mama started to cry. But she was smiling at the same time. "I'm so proud of you, Louis Daniel," she said.

"The buses are here!" someone yelled.
People pushed and shoved, trying to reach
the doors.

When we finally stepped outside, it
was so bright I had to blink a few times
before I could see. And there was that
black and white dog, wagging his tail
at me.

"Daddy, look!" I cried. "Please, please,
can we keep him?"

"Louis, we can't take a dog with us,"
he said. "The buses are for people."

"Who says we're going on any bus?"
Mama said.

Daddy looked at her for a long minute.

Then he smiled.

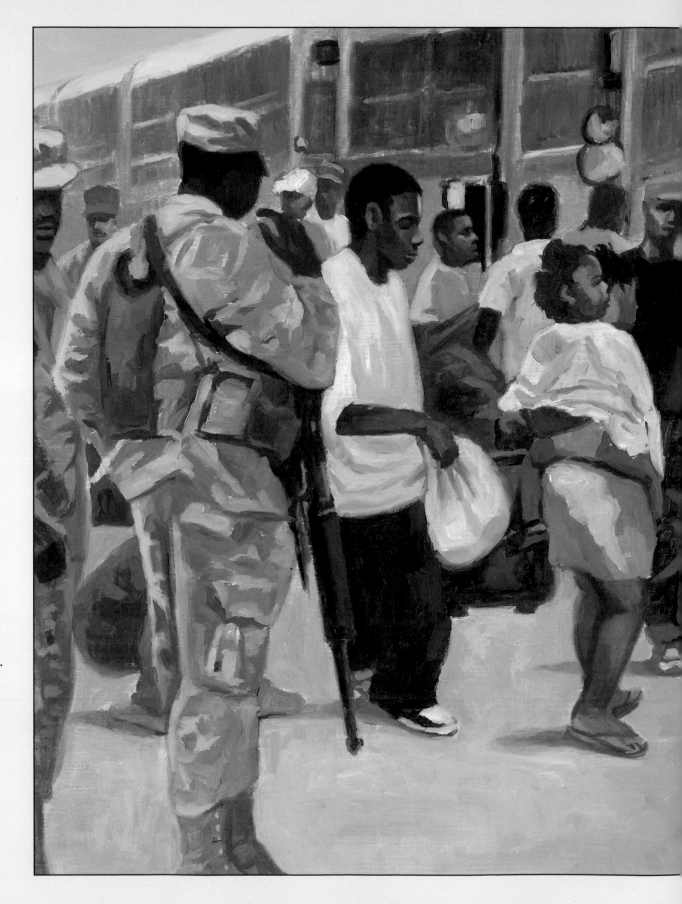

"Come on, boy," I said.

"We're going home."

Louis Daniel and his family are fictional characters. But what they experienced in this story is based on truth.

EARLY ON THE MORNING of August 29, 2005, a hurricane named Katrina came barreling out of the Gulf of Mexico with the seeming force of 10,000 freight trains. It was headed straight for New Orleans, Louisiana, a low-lying city protected from flooding by a system of levees and canals.

Packing winds up to 140 miles per hour, Katrina pushed huge waves into the Louisiana coast, flattening everything in its path. Then, racing across the flat marshland in minutes, Katrina found the mouth of the mighty Mississippi River. The storm hurled a powerful surge of water back up the river and into Lake Pontchartrain, already swollen with rainwater.

Within hours, Lake Borgne on the east and Lake Pontchartrain on the north overtopped their levees, while the general force of the water burst the walls of five major canals. Soon most of the city was submerged under seven feet of water. By the next morning, 80 percent of New Orleans was under water, in some places over twenty feet deep.

Boy playing on the field in the Superdome during the post-Katrina floods

Like Louis and his family in this story, thousands of people sought refuge from the rising waters and fled to the shelter that had been set up in the Superdome.

Katrina was the third strongest storm ever to make landfall in the United States, killing more than 1800 people. Approximately 850,000 housing units were damaged or destroyed.

Damage to the levees causes flooding in low-lying New Orleans neighborhoods

People wading through the New Orleans flood waters to get to higher ground

I consulted many books and websites as I developed Louis Daniel's story. Here are a few that were especially helpful.

BOOKS

BREACH OF FAITH: HURRICANE KATRINA AND THE NEAR DEATH OF A GREAT AMERICAN CITY by Jed Horne. Random House, 2006.

THE GREAT DELUGE: HURRICANE KATRINA, NEW ORLEANS, AND THE MISSISSIPPI GULF COAST by Douglas Brinkley. Harper Perennial, 2007.

PAWPRINTS OF KATRINA: PETS SAVED AND LESSONS LEARNED by Cathy Scott. Wiley Publishing, Inc., 2008.

LOUIS ARMSTRONG, IN HIS OWN WORDS: SELECTED WRITINGS by Louis Armstrong (Thomas Brothers, ed.). Oxford University Press, 1999.

WEBSITES

www.PBS.org/wgbh/nova/orleans

www.nhc.noaa.gov/outreach/history/#katrina

www.katrinadestruction.com

DVD

WHEN THE LEVEES BROKE: A REQUIEM IN FOUR ACTS, by Spike Lee. HBO Documentary, 2006.

To all the brave children of Katrina

—M. U.

For the communities devastated by Katrina and for their hope and spirit of rebuilding

And I would especially like to thank young Leon, his mother Susette, and my cousin Dexter St. Louis for making the family in this story come to life.

—C. B.

Published by
PEACHTREE PUBLISHERS
1700 Chattahoochee Avenue
Atlanta, Georgia 30318-2112
www.peachtree-online.com

Text © 2011 by Myron Uhlberg
Illustrations © 2011 by Colin Bootman
Photos on page 38 bottom and pages 39–40: FEMA images supplied by Illinois Photos; photo on page 38 top: John Rowland for Advertiser Media Network

Illustrations rendered in oil on prepared wood panels; title typeset in You Are Loved by Kimberly Geswein; text typeset in Monotype Corporation's Goudy Old Style Infant

Printed in November 2017 by Tien Wah Press in Malaysia

10 9 8 7 6 (hardcover)
10 9 8 7 6 5 4 3 (trade paperback)

HC: 978-1-56145-591-1
TPB: 978-1-56145-887-5

Library of Congress Cataloging-in-Publication Data

Uhlberg, Myron.
A storm called Katrina / written by Myron Uhlberg ; illustrated by Colin Bootman.
p. cm.
Summary: When flood waters submerge their New Orleans neighborhood in the aftermath of Hurricane Katrina, a young cornet player and his parents evacuate their home and struggle to survive and stay together.
ISBN 978-1-56145-591-1
1. Hurricane Katrina, 2005—Juvenile fiction. [1. Hurricane Katrina, 2005—Fiction. 2. Floods—Fiction. 3. Survival—Fiction. 4. African Americans—Fiction. 5. New Orleans (La.)—Fiction.] I. Bootman, Colin, ill. II. Title.
PZ7.U3257St 2010
[E]—dc22
2009024518

A stray dog walks the watery streets in New Orleans after the storm

Tens of thousands of cats and dogs were also affected. The Louisiana Society for the Prevention of Cruelty to Animals estimated that 70,000 pets remained in the city during the storm. About 15,000 were rescued and only 20 percent were reunited with their owners.

Before—and after—the storm hit, many people left New Orleans. Some of them never returned. Katrina's victims are now spread clear across America, from Texas to California, from North Dakota to Georgia.

But like Louis Daniel and his family, many others remained—and after the waters drained away, more residents returned. Their home is with their families in New Orleans, the birthplace of the great Louis Daniel Armstrong, who—like the fictional Louis Daniel of this story—once blew his horn in his beloved hometown, with joy and hope for the future.

If you'd like to know more about Hurricane Katrina, you might want to check out these resources.

BOOKS

HURRICANE KATRINA (TURNING POINTS IN U.S. HISTORY) by Judith Bloom Fradin and Dennis Brindell Fradin. Cavendish Square Publishing, 2009.

HURRICANE KATRINA AND THE DEVASTATION OF NEW ORLEANS (MONUMENTAL MILESTONES) by John A. Torres. Mitchell Lane Publishers, 2006.

HURRICANES: THE SCIENCE BEHIND KILLER STORMS by Alvin Silverstein, Virginia Silverstein, and Laura Silverstein Nunn. Enslow Publishers, 2009.

HURRICANES: WITNESS TO DISASTER by Judy and Dennis Fradin. National Geographic, 2007.

WEBSITES

www.katrinaschildren.com
Information on *Katrina's Children,* a documentary film about nineteen children from different neighborhoods of New Orleans

kids.niehs.nih.gov/explore/nworld/hurricane_katrina.htm
The National Institute of Environmental Health Sciences Kids' Pages about Hurricane Katrina and environmental health and safety

www.teachervision.fen.com/hurricane/resource/34251.html
Printables, articles, and references to help students understand the devastation caused by Hurricane Katrina